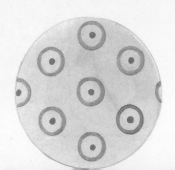

FUNDED BY A
GRANT FROM
ConocoPhillips

BiG RED LoLLiPoP

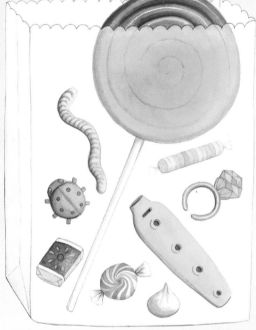

by Rukhsana Khan

illustrated by Sophie Blackall

Viking

An Imprint of Penguin Group (USA) Inc.

For Tariq and Aisha Van der Loo, and in memory of their mother, my sister Bushra—R.K.

For Olive—S.B.

Viking
Published by Penguin Group
Penguin Young Readers Group, 345 Hudson Street, New York, New York 10014, U.S.A.
Penguin Group (Canada), 90 Eglinton Avenue East, Suite 700, Toronto, Ontario, Canada M4P 2Y3 (a division of Pearson Penguin Canada Inc.)
Penguin Books Ltd, 80 Strand, London WC2R 0RL, England
Penguin Ireland, 25 St Stephen's Green, Dublin 2, Ireland (a division of Penguin Books Ltd)
Penguin Group (Australia), 250 Camberwell Road, Camberwell, Victoria 3124, Australia (a division of Pearson Australia Group Pty Ltd)
Penguin Books India Pvt Ltd, 11 Community Centre, Panchsheel Park, New Delhi – 110 017, India
Penguin Group (NZ), 67 Apollo Drive, Rosedale, North Shore 0745, Auckland, New Zealand (a division of Pearson New Zealand Ltd.)
Penguin Books (South Africa) (Pty) Ltd, 24 Sturdee Avenue, Rosebank, Johannesburg 2196, South Africa

Penguin Books Ltd, Registered Offices: 80 Strand, London WC2R 0RL, England

First published in 2010 by Viking, a division of Penguin Young Readers Group

1   3   5   7   9   10   8   6   4   2

Text copyright © Rukhsana Khan, 2010
Illustrations copyright © Sophie Blackall, 2010
All rights reserved

LIBRARY OF CONGRESS CATALOGING-IN-PUBLICATION DATA
Khan, Rukhsana, 1962–
Big red lollipop / by Rukhsana Khan ; illustrated by Sophie Blackall.
p. cm.
Summary: Having to take her younger sister along the first time she is invited to a birthday party spoils Rubina's fun, and later when
that sister is asked to a party and baby sister wants to come, Rubina must decide whether to help.
ISBN 978-0-670-06287-4 (hardcover)
[1. Sisters—Fiction. 2. Birthdays—Fiction. 3. Parties—Fiction. 4. Conduct of life—Fiction. 5. Arab Americans—Fiction.]
I. Blackall, Sophie, ill. II. Title.
PZ7.K52654Big 2010   [E]—dc22   2009022676

Manufactured in China   Set in Elysium   Book design by Nancy Brennan

I'm so excited I run all the way   home from school.

"Ami! I've been invited to a birthday party! There's going to be games and toys, cake and ice cream! Can I go?"

Sana screams, "I wanna go too!"

Ami says, "What's a birthday party?"

"It's when they celebrate the day they were born."

"Why do they do *that*?"

"They just do! Can I go?"

Sana screams, "I wanna go too!"

"I can't take *her*! She's not invited."

"Why not?" says Ami.

"They don't do that here!"

Ami says, "Well that's not fair. You call up your friend and ask if you can bring Sana, or else you can't go."

"But Ami! They'll laugh at me! They'll never invite me to another party again!"

Sana screams, "I wanna go too!"

I say, "Look, Sana, one day you'll get invited to your own friends' parties. Wouldn't you like that better?"

"No! I wanna go now!"

I beg and plead, but Ami won't listen. I have no choice. I have to call. Sally says, "All right." But it doesn't sound all right. I know she thinks I'm weird.

At the party, I'm the only one who brought
her little sister. Sana has to win all the
games, and when she falls down
during musical chairs, she cries
like a baby.

Before we leave the party, Sally's mom gives us little bags.

Inside there are chocolates and candies, a whistle,
a ruby ring, and a big red lollipop! Sana eats her big
red lollipop on the way home in the car. I save mine
for later.

Sana doesn't know how to make things last. By bedtime,
her candies are all gone, her whistle is broken, and the ruby
in her ring is missing. I put my big red lollipop on the top
shelf of the fridge to have in the morning.

All night I dream about how good it will taste.

In the morning, I get up early to have it. Sana's already up. When she sees me, she runs away.

I open the fridge door. All that's left of my lollipop is a triangle stuck to a stick.

"SANA!"

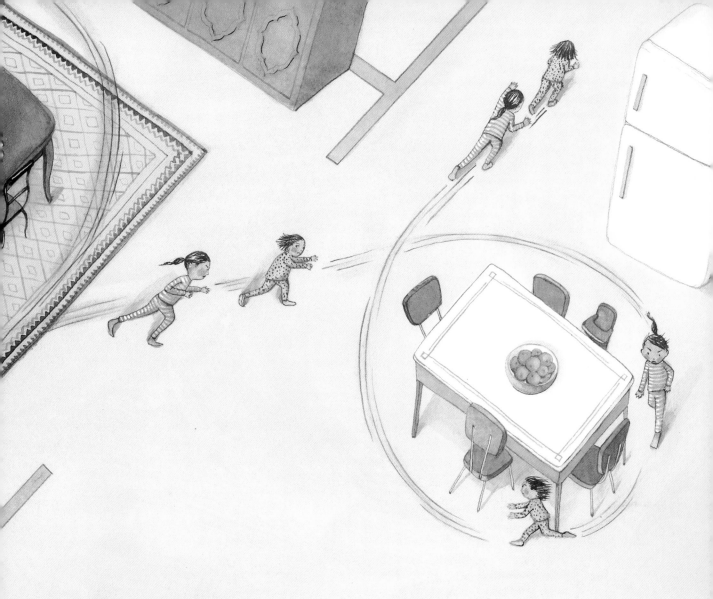

I hear a sound in the front hall closet. I should have known. That's where she always hides.

I shove aside the coats and boots. "I'm going to *get* you!"

Quick as a rat, she scoots through my legs and runs around and around the living room, the dining room, the kitchen, yelling, "Ami! Ami! Help! Help!"

Ami comes out, rubbing her eyes. Sana runs behind Ami, where I can't get her.

"What's going on out here?" says Ami.

Sana says, "Rubina's trying to get me!"

Ami puts her hands on her hips. "Are you trying to get your little sister again?"

"She ate my *lollipop*! The greedy thing! She ate it!"

Ami says, "For shame! It's just a lollipop! Can't you *share* with your little sister?"

I want to cry, but I don't.

Sana runs to the fridge and brings back the triangle
stuck to the stick. "Look! I didn't eat *all* of your lollipop!
I left the triangle for you!"

"See?" says Ami. "She didn't eat *all* of it. She's
sharing with you! Go ahead. Take the triangle."
So I have to take it.

"Go ahead. *Eat* the triangle."

But I don't. With all my might, I throw it across the
room. It skitters under the sofa.

Sana scurries after it and eats that too.

The worst thing is that all the girls at school
know if they invite me to their birthday parties,
I have to bring Sana.

I don't get any invitations for a really long time.

Then one day Sana comes home waving an invitation. "Ami! I've been invited to a birthday party! There's going to be games and toys and cake and ice cream! Can I go?"

Our little sister Maryam screams, "I wanna go too!"
Sana says, "No! I can't take *her*! She's not invited!"

Ami says, "Well . . . it's only fair. You went to Rubina's friend's party, now Rubina and Maryam can go to your friend's party."

I say, "Leave me out of it."

Ami says, "Fine then, you have to take Maryam."

Now it's Sana's turn to beg and plead. Ami won't listen. Sana's begging so hard she's crying, but still Ami won't listen.

I *could* just watch her have to take Maryam. I *could* just let her make a fool of herself at that party. I *could* just let her not be invited to any more parties, but something makes me tap Ami on the shoulder.

"What?"

"Don't make Sana take Maryam to the party."

"No?" says Ami.

"No," I say.

Ami thinks for a moment, then says, "Okay."

So Sana gets to go by herself.

After the party, I hear a knock
on my door.

"What do *you* want?" I ask Sana.

"Here." She hands me a big green
lollipop. "This is for you."

"Thanks," I say.

After that we're friends.